THE BOY AND THE GOATS

THE BOY
AND THE GOATS

Margaret Hillert

Illustrated by Yoshi Miyake

Library of Congress Cataloging in Publication Data

Hillert, Margaret.
    The boy and the goats.

    (MCP beginning-to-read books)

    SUMMARY: When a boy can not retrieve his goats
from a neighboring field, a rabbit, fox, wolf, and
bee come to his aid. Only one of them is successful.
    [1. Folklore]   I. Miyake, Yoshi.   II. Title.
PZ8.1.H539Bo   398.2′45297358   [E]   80–20840

ISBN 0-8136-5592-7   Paperback
ISBN 0-8136-5092-5   Hardbound

            14 15 16 17 18 19 20   02 01 00

Come, goats.
Come with me.
We will go for a walk and
find something for you to eat.

This is a good spot.
You can eat here.
Eat, eat, eat.

Oh, oh.
Do not do that.
You can not eat that.
Jump out. Jump out.

Oh, no!
Not you, too.
This will not do.
Get out! Get out!

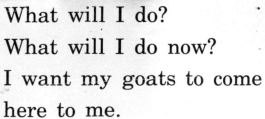

What will I do?
What will I do now?
I want my goats to come
here to me.

What is it, little boy?
What is it?
Can I help you?

My goats will not come out.
What can you do?
How can you help?

I will run at the goats.
Look what I can do.

Oh, no.

That did not work, did it?

That did not work.

Oh, my. Oh, my.
What have we here?
What is it, you two?

We can not make my
goats come out.
Look at that.
The goats will not jump out.

I will help you.

See me run at the goats.

I guess it did not work.
I am no help to you.

My, my.

Look at you three.

How funny you look.

What is it?

My goats eat and eat and
will not come here to me.
What am I to do?

Oh, I will work for you.
I will help.
This is something I am good at.
Go, goats, go.

Oh, my!
The goats did not go out.
What can I do now?

Here. Here.
What is it?
You do not look good.

My goats will not come to me.
No one can help me.
What am I to do?

I can help you.
I can make the goats come out.
Do you want me to help?

You!
You are funny.
How can you make the
goats come out?
You are too little.

You will see.
I am little, but I can do it.
Here I go.

And here come my goats.
You did it!
You did it!
Oh, you are good.

Come, goats.
Come on. Come on.
You are out, and we can go now.

Margaret Hillert, author of several books in the MCP Beginning-To-Read Series, is a writer, poet, and teacher.

The Boy and the Goats uses the 59 words listed below.

a	get	make	that
am	go	me	the
and	goats	my	this
are	good		three
at	guess	no	to
		not	too
boy	have	now	two
but	help		
	here	oh	walk
can	how	on	want
come		one	we
	I	out	what
did	is		will
do	it	run	with
			work
eat	jump	see	
		something	you
find	little	spot	
for	look		
funny			